THE MOUSE IN THE MATZAH FACTORY

by

Francine Medoff

illustrated by

David Goldstein

KAR-BEN COPIES, INC.   **ROCKVILLE, MD**

ABOUT MATZAH

Matzah, unleavened bread eaten during the Passover holiday, recalls the bread the Jews ate in their hasty flight from Egypt. Wheat used to make matzah is carefully protected against contact with water and heat which could cause leavening. No more than 18 minutes may elapse from the time the water and flour are combined until the matzah is baked. Wheat for the ordinary, machine-made Passover matzah found on grocery shelves is watched from the time of milling. Wheat for *shmurah* matzah—special matzah often made by hand—is watched from harvest time.

Library of Congress Cataloging in Publication Data

Medoff, Francine.
    The mouse in the matzah factory.

    Summary: A mouse observes wheat being harvested, ground into flour, mixed into dough, and baked into matzah.
    [1. Mice—Fiction. 2. Matzos—Fiction. 3. Jews—Rites and ceremonies—Fiction] I. Goldstein, David, 1948-   ill. II. Title.
PZ7.M51277Mo 1983   [E]   82-23349
ISBN 0-930494-19-9 (pbk.)

Once there was a little mouse who lived in a wheat field in the country.

One day men came and built a fence around the wheat field. Every day they watched over the growing wheat. They watered the field, pulled the weeds, and waited for the wheat to ripen. The little mouse watched, too. He wondered what was so special about this wheat.

When the wheat was ripe, the men cut it down. They worked carefully, making sure to keep the wheat dry. They tied it in bundles and loaded it onto a wagon.

The mouse decided to follow the wheat.

Soon the wagon arrived at the mill. The mouse poked around until he found a hole in the bottom of the door. He crept inside. Huge grinding wheels were crushing the wheat into fine flour. The millers carefully poured the flour into brand new sacks and loaded them onto a truck.

The mouse jumped aboard the truck and hid among the sacks, wondering where the truck would take them. They drove for a long time. They left the country, with its open fields and wide spaces, and came to the city. The little mouse peeked out. He saw tall buildings. He saw crowds of people. He heard the noise of cars and trucks on the street.

At last, the truck stopped in front of an old building. Workers came to unload the sacks of flour. Quickly and quietly, the mouse jumped down and followed.

An inspector stood at the door, checking to see that each flour sack was dry and tightly closed.

The mouse was afraid he would be discovered, so he climbed onto a window ledge, squeezed through a crack, and hid behind a clock.

He saw a large room with many people.
They were all very busy.

In one area, workers were unloading the sacks of flour. In another place, they were bringing in buckets of water. In the middle was a man with a mixing bowl.

When the mixing man called out, the flour man scooped a cup of flour from the sack, reached through a little window, and dumped the flour into a bowl.

When the mixing man called out again, the water man filled his pitcher with water, passed it through his window, and poured the water into the bowl.

The mixing man worked very quickly, mixing the flour and water into a lump of dough. The little mouse watched. He wondered what was so special about this dough.

The mixing man brought the dough to another
area, where many people stood at a long table.
He gave a piece of dough to each person. They
quickly rolled their dough into circles.

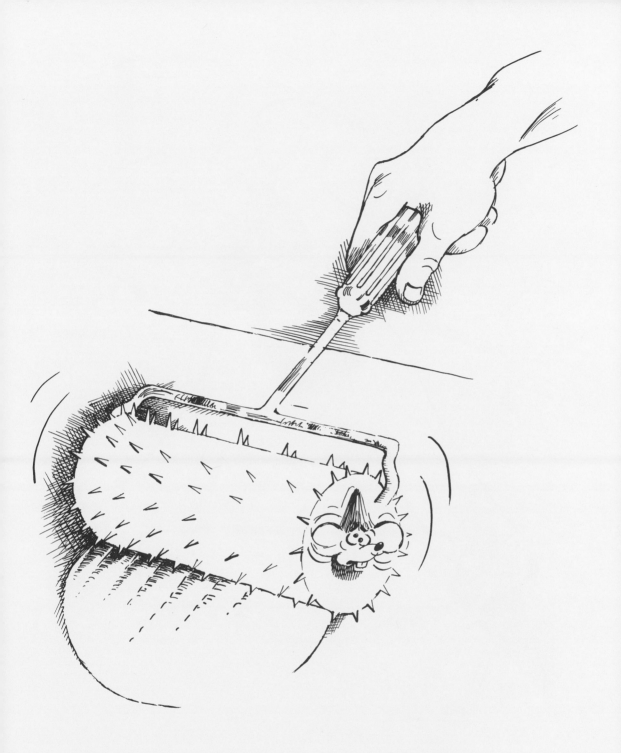

The circles were passed to another table, where a man poked holes into them with a special tool. He lined up the circles on a rack near a brick oven.

The baker slid the circles into the oven. Minutes later, they were crisp and brown. A delicious smell filled the room as he took them out of the oven and placed them on a rolling cart.

All of a sudden a bell rang. The people began to clean their work areas. They scrubbed the tables, sanded down the rolling pins, and washed and dried the bowls. When they were finished, the mixing man reset the clock and called out for more flour and water.

The mouse couldn't resist the delicious smell. He followed the cart into a room where people were packing the baked circles into boxes and tying them with string. Families were standing in line to buy the boxes.

He hopped onto the counter to take a peek.

This is what he read:

"That's right!" the mouse thought. "I watched this matzah. I watched it from the time the wheat began to grow in my wheat field."

I watched it being harvested.

I watched it being ground into flour.

I watched it being mixed into dough.

I watched it being baked into matzah.

The mouse felt very important. He decided it was time to return to the country. Soon more wheat would be planted, and he wanted to be home in time to watch it again.